DATE DUE

A Giant First-Start Reader

This easy reader contains only 40 different words,
repeated often to help the young reader develop
word recognition and interest in reading.

Basic word list for *Little Christmas Elf*

a	everybody	needs
all	for	now
and	full	of
are	he	oh
at	help	Santa
bang	here	Santa's
busy	ho	Simon
Christmas	hurray	tap
clink	is	the
clunk	little	these
comes	look	this
crash	lot	toys
elves	merry	will
		workshop

Little Christmas Elf

Written by Eileen Curran

Illustrated by Don Page

Troll Associates

Library of Congress Cataloging in Publication Data

Curran, Eileen.
    Little Christmas elf.

    Summary: Little Simon the elf is not a very efficient
worker in Santa's workshop until he gets help from
Santa Claus himself.
    1. Children's stories, American. [1. Santa Claus—
Fiction. 2. Christmas—Fiction] I. Page, Don,
1946-   ill.   II. Title.
PZ7.C9298Li   1985   [E]   84-8628
ISBN 0-8167-0352-3 (lib. bdg.)

Tap, tap, tap. This is Santa's Workshop.

Bang, bang, bang.

These are Santa's elves.

Clink, clink, clink.

This is little Simon.

He needs help.

Clunk, clunk, clunk.
Oh...little Simon needs a lot of help!

Tap, tap, tap.

Look at all the busy elves.

Bang, bang, bang.

Look at all the toys.

Clink, clink, clink.
Look at little Simon.

Oh...clunk, clunk, clunk.
Simon needs a little help!

Ho, ho, ho! Here comes Santa.

Oh, oh! And here comes little Simon.

Oh...crash! Bang!
Oh, help!

Will Santa help Simon?

Look at little Simon now.
Tap, tap…
Bang, bang…

Tap, tap, tap. Santa's Workshop is full now.

Bang, bang, bang. Look at all the toys.

"Hurray for little Simon!"

"Hurray for Santa!"

"Merry Christmas, everybody!"